Fiona the Theater Mouse

by

Sheila Murray-Nellis

Eva Nova Press
P.O. Box 313
Kaslo, BC V0G 1M0

ISBN 978-0-9691917-5-9

For Lila Marie and Maëlenn Louise
and for Patrick, my first reader

Forward

When my sons were in high school in Woodstock, Vermont, their theater group was chosen as one of two U.S. high school theater programs to perform at the Fringe Theatre Festival in Edinburgh, Scotland. On returning to North America, their director, Harriet Worrell, toyed with the idea of adding "Brigadoon" to their upcoming season, capitalizing on the students' Scotland experience.

Although Harriet eventually decided against staging "Brigadoon," my niece, who lived in another state, was cast as Fiona in her own high school production of the play that year. This was the context in which the first draft of Fiona the Theater Mouse was written.

I want to thank Harriet Worrell for all the wonderful work she has done with students, including my three sons, over the years. She has truly been an inspiration to so many of them.

I thank all three of my sons, as well -- Aaron, Brendan, and Patrick -- for the fun moments watching them on stage.

And here's to Caitlin Molly Thurnauer, my niece, now launched in her professional acting career.

I love you all!

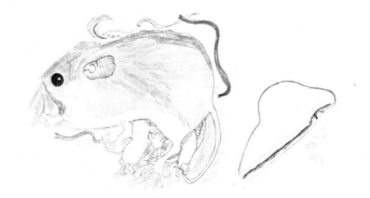

Table of Contents

Chapter 1

Mouse in Residence

No one in the Noodle Soup Community Theater knew about the mouse family living behind the dressing room wall, but Wilson, the janitor, had his suspicions. He was annoyed by the little black droppings he sometimes found under the counter and behind the hat rack.

"But you see, the traps are always empty," he said to himself with a chuckle. "I guess I've sent them packing."

Fat chance that. Ma Mouse would not budge. She stayed in her cozy corner even after her dear late husband was fooled into eating peanut butter smeared on a rickety trap. She had even given birth to a whole new generation of mice that were nicely settled in their nest of cloth scraps, ribbons, and hat feathers.

One day, as Ma was gazing at her babies lovingly, the director of the Noodle Soup Community Theater called out the names of the characters in the humans' upcoming play, "Brigadoon."

Ma nodded her head. "Wouldn't their Daddy be pleased as punch to see them now! And what pretty names -- Jean, Charlie, Tommy, Jeff, Jane, Andrew, and Fiona. Daddy always did like the theater!"

As the days passed, the baby mice became so used to hearing the theater director call out their names that they stopped taking notice. All, that is, except Fiona, whose ears pricked up whenever she heard her name.

"Ma, have you ever wanted to dance on stage?" Fiona asked one day after Ma had just shown them all her best pirouette.

Ma looked at her daughter sternly and said, "Fig juice! Don't be silly! And don't any of you even think about wandering onto that stage! Humans are dangerous. You can never tell what they might do."

All of the youngsters obeyed their mother -- all, that is, except Fiona.

Fiona meant to obey. But then the music started up. Ma and her other young mice, each of whose fur was starting to fill in nicely, twirled around and around until one mouse bumped into another. Someone started to bicker. A third mouse shouted when somebody stepped on his tail. The space felt so stuffy that Fiona squeezed through a chink in the wall to get a breath of fresh air.

Outside the nest, Fiona found even more confusion. She kept to the edge of the wall, of course, the way her mother had taught her to do when they went night foraging. Only this time there were people around.

One kept calling to another, "Fiona! Fiona has to be ready to come on stage at a moment's notice! If you are not ready, there are plenty of others who'd love to be Fiona!"

Fiona Mouse sat back on her haunches. "I had no idea," she whispered to herself, "that so many others would love to be me!"

Fiona couldn't resist following the two women out of the costume room and then backstage where, quick as a lick, Fiona scooted under the green folds of the velvet curtain. From there, she could watch the humans dance.

Fiona felt a tickle in her tummy. The huge legs of the people kicked and leapt into the air the same way that Ma had taught Fiona and her brothers and sisters to do. And the songs they sang were the same songs that Ma sang when tucking them into the nest for a nap.

Nobody bothered about the curtain Fiona had rolled herself in. Then a man came on stage and began to sing a rousing version of "I'll Go Home with Bonny Jean." Even though he kicked and hopped as he belted out the song, Fiona was so tired that she let herself be lulled to sleep.

When she awoke, the stage was empty. Everything was quiet. She tried to untangle herself from the curtain, but no matter how she pulled and tugged, her paws got all tangled up and stuck.

Fiona started to panic. She gave one more yank and the curtain underneath her came loose. She went tumbling across the stage and over the edge with a thump. "Ow!" she squeaked from underneath the front row seat.

It was probably just around then, after she had licked the bump on her back leg, that Fiona looked up and saw someone swooping overhead.

Chapter 2

A Friend with Wings

A small brown someone swooped down from the rafters, letting out a series of high-pitched squeaks. He swerved towards the window and landed on the sill.

"Hello?" he said. "Who's there? Hmm, you'd have to be a pretty big bug to make that kind of crash!"

Fiona giggled. "Down here. I'm on the floor." She sat up straight. "My name's Fiona. I'm not a bug. I'm a mouse."

"A mouse? What's that?" The fuzzy brown creature flapped down and landed on the armrest. He twirled over the edge and hung upside down. "I'm Bart." He was still for a moment. Then he whispered, "What happened to your wings?"

"What wings?" Fiona wrinkled her nose as she looked straight at him.

"You mean you've never had any?" Bart squeaked a little louder.

"Of course not! None of my family has wings." Fiona carefully studied the way the furry creature's leathery wings folded about his body. "Where did you get yours?"

"Oh, I was born with them, I guess." Bart adjusted himself on the armrest. "I've never known a bat without them before."

"But I'm not a bat!" said Fiona. "I've told you. I'm a mouse."

"Oh," said Bart. "I'm sorry."

"What for? I like being a mouse." Fiona flicked her whiskers.

"You do?" Bart sounded surprised. "Hmm, how do you fly around and get bugs, then? You must be very hungry."

"Bugs? Yuck! I eat crumbs and seeds and stuff, like this." Fiona picked up a stale kernel of popcorn someone had dropped beneath the seat. She held it out to him. "Would you like to try some? It's delicious!"

Bart sniffed it. "Eeeew! No thanks."

Bart flew up, searching for the tasty moth fluttering by the window. He finally caught it with his sticky tongue. Then he flew back. "Now that was delicious!" he said.

He nodded to Fiona shyly. She realized she had been staring at him. Then he said, "I've never noticed you here before. Have you been here long?"

"Only all of my life," she replied. "But we mice try to be quiet. The humans, you know."

"Oh, them," he said. "Yeah, I know what you mean. They don't like me very much either. But how about it? You and I -- we could be friends, couldn't we?"

"Yes, I'd like that," Fiona said.

"Come on, then!" Bart flew up to the rafters, then around the vast room, doing flips and loop-de-loops. "Come on, Fiona!"

Fiona rolled her eyes. "Now, how am I supposed to do that?"

"Oh," he said. He swooped down, landing where she sat on her haunches. "Sorry, I forgot. Here, jump up on my back."

When Fiona had settled herself between his wings, Bart gave a high-pitched squeak. "Now hold on tight!" Bart lifted into the air. His body jerked from side to side. Then, just before they crashed into the post, he swerved aside.

Fiona was terrified. She dug her claws deeper and deeper into his fur.

"Ouch!" Bart said. "Not so hard. Just relax a little."

Fiona shut her eyes tightly the first time she thought they were going to crash into the wall. When she opened them a slit, they were a few inches from a light bulb. Now she opened one eye a little wider. There, she thought, taking a deep breath. We haven't crashed after all. What am I so afraid of?

Fiona saw to her dismay that they were higher off the ground than she had ever been before. But what a view! Instead of seeing only a few inches in all directions, which is how it is when you are only an inch from the ground, she could now see the entire theater -- the stage, the seats, the entrance to the lobby.

"You can see so much from up here!" Fiona exclaimed.

"See? What do you mean?" Bart expertly maneuvered between posts and rafters.

Fiona looked around excitedly. "From up here, you can look down on everything!"

"You mean hear their echoes," said Bart. "Yes, I can tell how high up we are, how far away we are from each wall, and where each tasty bug is hiding."

"You hear their what?" Fiona felt the fur on her neck start to rise. She squeezed more tightly.

"Echoes. I use echo location. You mean, you don't have that either?"

"Don't you see how far away things are with your eyes?" Fiona squeaked softly.

"My eyes? Eyes, whoopie pies!" said Bart. "Why, they're not as useful to me as echo location."

"You mean, you're blind?" asked Fiona.

"Well, not exactly blind . . . ."

"Blind as a bat? Oh, my goodness! I'm flying up here, a hundred miles from the floor, with a blind bat who almost bumped into that post a moment ago. Oh, help! Get me down! Get me down!" Fiona squeaked pitifully and squirmed higher and higher on his back.

"Would you quit it?" Bart said as he landed on the stage. "And we weren't a hundred miles up. We were only twenty-four and a half feet up. I told you -- I use echo location, which is apparently much more accurate than eyes for measuring distance and for judging stuff. And I can see, too. How else did you think I knew you didn't have any wings?"

Fiona tumbled over his shoulders onto the stage. "Whew!" she sighed. "We're safe!"

"Of course, we're safe." Bart fluttered away.

Fiona scurried under the curtains and sniffed her way to where her mother was searching frantically for her.

Chapter 3

A Mother's Perspective

Ma was running around in circles, looking for her little mouse. "Oh, I thought I'd lost you for good!" she exclaimed on seeing her daughter. "Where, in heaven's name, have you been? Those horrid human traps could be lurking anywhere, luring you with a smear of peanut butter or a hunk of smelly cheese! You must be more careful, dear." Her mother sniffed Fiona. Then she sat up on her hind legs and sniffed the air.

"Oh, Ma," said Fiona. "I've made a new friend. He's a bat named Bart."

"Huh!" Ma poked her nose into Fiona's back and started to lick her clean. "Bats can't even see."

"Yes, but he flew me as high as the ceiling. I could see everything from up there."

"I'm not sure you should trust a non-mouse," said her mother. "You just can't be sure what they might be thinking. And then there's the fact of their wings . . . ."

"But, Ma, his wings help him fly way up into the air . . . ."

"Imagine having something so bird-like. And do you have any idea what bats eat?"

"Ma, he's my friend," said Fiona.

"Let's get back to the nest. I've left all your brothers and sisters alone. They may have everything torn up by now."

Ma's worries were not exaggerated. When Fiona and her mother entered the nest, feathers were scattered and drifting in the air. Fabric scraps and ribbons lay strewn about.

"Ma, Charlie nipped my tail," said Jean.

"But she tickled me with her whiskers first!" Charlie nudged between two of his sisters.

Meg pushed him aside. "They made so much noise, they woke me up," she complained.

"Children, can't I leave you for just a few minutes without your squabbling?" demanded their mother.

"Now settle down and find your places in the nest." She fluffed up the scraps and ribbons. "We've had a night of foraging, and I just saw the light coming in through the window. The humans will be back soon. It's time for you all to get to sleep."

The young mice scrambled for places closest to their mother and then settled down in the soft pile of fabric. Soon they were all fast asleep.

All, that is, except Fiona.

Chapter 4

A Two-Headed Bat

No matter how she tried to curl up among her brothers and sisters, Fiona could not get to sleep. She could hear the heavy breathing of her mother and the rhythmic rise and fall of her siblings' breath. She really did try to fall in with the sound, letting her own breath match theirs, but it was no use! Maybe if she could move around a little, she thought, get some exercise and a bit of fresh air.

Fiona sniffed her way out of the mouse hole and into the closet. The hems of the dresses and the cuffs of the men's trousers tickled her back as she passed. She crept past brown shoes with laces, medium sized black shoes with chunky heels, and small red shoes with pointy toes. A leather belt had slipped from a pair of pants and lay curled in a corner like a snake. Fiona shivered. A jumble of bows and ruffles, suspenders and striped ties lay in a heap just inside the closet door. This door hung limply on its hinges and creaked whenever someone opened the big door to the outside and set a draft moving through the room.

Fiona kept close to the wall, the way her mother had taught her. She squeezed carefully through the space under the door and into the corridor. She ran across the floor and through the stage door, then ducked behind the green velvet curtain.

Just then, the door to the outside flew open. A woman swinging a large cloth bag burst through. The door in the costume room creaked on its hinges. Fiona wondered whether the sound would wake her mother and what her mother would say this time when Fiona returned to the nest.

Fiona looked up and saw her friend high in the rafters, wrapped in his leathery wings and hanging upside down. His drowsy voice warned her, "Look out! Humans approach!"

Fiona curled up in the curtain's folds. As she settled in, the night's adventures began to catch up with her. She felt her eyelids get heavier and heavier.

Then she was jolted awake. Someone was yanking the curtain from underneath her. She ran around and around in circles, then clutched the curtain's bottom with her claws.

"Climb up!" called Bart from above. She saw his eyes blink beneath his folded wings. "Climb up the curtain!"

Without stopping to think what she was doing, Fiona climbed up the curtain farther and farther. The curtain was still moving across the stage, so she clung more tightly for fear of being flung off. She climbed even faster. She stopped when she was high over the stage where the curtain was attached to ropes and pulleys. Suddenly, the curtain she was clinging to stopped moving. The wooden floor below looked very hard and very, very far away.

Fiona saw Bart unwrap his wings and flap over to her. He perched close beside her on the curtain top. "Don't be afraid, Fiona," he said. "It's rather nice up here."

"What do I do now?" she replied. "I don't have any wings, you know." The fur lifted from her neck, and she was trembling.

"Here, crawl onto my back the way you did last night. I won't let you fall."

Fiona eased herself onto Bart's back between his wings. She crawled up so that her head was just above his.

"We've got to get out of this light. It makes me weak. Now get ready -- here we go!" cried Bart.

"Be careful! The humans . . ." squeaked Fiona.

But it was too late. When Bart dove down with Fiona's extra weight on his back, he went a little lower than he'd ordinarily go.

One of the dancers saw them and began to scream. "A bat!" she yelled. "A bat with two heads!"

"Now Marcy, don't be ridiculous." said the director. "Bats have only one head, just like you and I do. We'll get the janitor to get rid of the bat this evening. Now let's do that number once again." The director rolled up her papers and tapped them against the palm of her hand.

"But I saw it, too. There were four beady little eyes!" cried Donna, another dancer.

"Ladies, we have less than twenty-four hours before show time. Now start from the top. No time for nonsense!"

Chapter 5

A Human Ambush

As the music began, Bart and Fiona watched from the rafters. Somewhere deep inside, Fiona felt the danger they were in.

"Let's hide up here," said Bart. He flew to a little hole over the stage. "Maybe you can watch and tell me what they're doing."

"Bart, do you think they can catch us up here?" Fiona was frantic.

"I don't think they'll bother us, at least not while they're dancing," answered Bart.

They heard the director arguing with the janitor. Only a few snippets of their conversation rose to their ears, but Fiona was sure she heard the words, ". . . can't have bats flying into the audience, Wilson, . . . upsetting people . . . might make the dancers trip . . . ."

And the janitor shaking his head. ". . . Try my best . . . hard to catch . . . don't know how he got in . . . ."

Fiona turned to Bart. "Have they ever seen you before?"

"The humans? Not that I know of," he replied. "Well, maybe once or twice. Enough for me to know they don't like me. I always make them scream. What are they doing now?"

"It's the sword dance. Have you ever seen it before? Or, you know, sensed it with your echo what-cha-ma-call-it?"

"With echo-location I can't tell exactly what they're doing. I can just tell their size, their movement, how far away they are, and whether they are, you know, good to eat."

"Oh, I doubt they're that." Fiona wrinkled her nose in distaste.

"I was just kidding about the good to eat part. They're too big, for one thing." Bart settled back against the wooden plank and sighed. "I'm a bug lover myself."

Fiona watched the men in their kilts perform the sword dance. As the dancers moved beneath, Fiona described their actions in detail to Bart. "Now they're hopping in a line! They're clanging their swords together." The swords flashed in the light when they lifted them high.

Then the dance was over. Soon the bustling humans gathered together their props and streamed off the stage. They left the building in twos and threes.

Suddenly some scuffling came from the costume room. "Eeee! A mouse!" shrieked a voice.

"Oh, oh. Must be Mama looking for me!" Fiona tightened her grasp on the hole's edge. "I hope they don't catch her," she whispered.

Fiona and Bart sat still. They heard a shuffling, some muttering, and then a final "That should do it!" Two women left the costume room and opened the door to the outside.

"First the two-headed bat -- I'll never forget the sight of that creature with all the eyes! Donna saw it, too -- and now this creepy little mouse! Margie, vermin are taking over the place! It's sickening," said one woman to the other. They slammed the door behind them.

When everything was quiet again, Bart turned to Fiona. "Time to get back down?"

"Oh, yes!" she replied. "I've got to check on my family." She squirmed onto his furry back. "You know what, Bart? Ma is great and all that, but she's not too fond of non-mice. Just in case she says something weird, I wanted you to know."

"Will she scream the way the humans do?"

"No, not like that, but she may squeak a lot and make me stay in the nest for a week or something."

Bart flapped down to the stage floor and Fiona slid off his back.

"I'll leave you here at the door, then," said Bart. "But you'll let me know if you need help?"

"Of course, I will. Thanks so much. And Bart? I've really enjoyed your company today."

Bart flew up and swooped from side to side, his movements like a joyful dance.

Fiona watched him fly through the doorway that led to the dark places behind the stage.

Fiona squeezed under the dressing room door and looked around. The room was shadowy as it usually was when the humans were gone.

Fiona remembered her mother's words the last time she returned to the mouse hole after meeting Bart. Ma had talked about human danger and not being fooled by smelly cheese.

Staying close to the walls, Fiona tiptoed past piles of costumes until she reached the open closet door. She had to tunnel through more ribbons and lace than were there earlier in the day. Up ahead was the mouse hole.

Outside a car passed, sending long fingers of light through the window and into the closet. Fiona saw a bright flash in front of the mouse hole. It reminded her of the swords on the stage. As she slowly approached, she saw a metal wire attached to a rectangular piece of wood a little longer than her body. It was right in front of the mouse hole, and in the center of it sat a hunk of delicious-smelling cheese.

Fiona remembered that she hadn't eaten all day.

Chapter 6

Courage

"Fiona!" She heard her mother's strained voice inside the mouse hole. "Don't come any closer. It's a human ambush! That's how your father lost his life. Stay away at all costs!"

"But Ma!" cried Fiona. "What will I do?"

"Child, you'll have to find somewhere else to hide," said her mother. "Go back and find that bat friend of yours. It's risky, but less risky than being at the mercy of the humans."

"But what about you?" Fiona looked at her mother's worried face. "If you can't come out, what will you eat?"

"Go, Fiona! We'll have to figure that out. But you must hurry. And Fiona, never, never, under any circumstances, go near one of these wood and metal contraptions!"

Fiona scurried out of the closet. She ran along the walls, under the door, and down the hall until she came to the back of the stage. There another surprise awaited her.

The entire stage was flooded with light.

Fiona looked up and saw Bart, perched helplessly with his head tucked under his wing. The light is working its spell on him, thought Fiona. "No, Bart, fly away!" she said.

Fiona saw the ladder set up beneath where Bart hung from the rafters and Wilson the janitor climbing the rungs with a net in one hand and the torn flap from a cardboard box in the other. He scooped the trembling Bart into the net and slapped the cardboard over the top. Bart clicked and squeaked trying to escape, but it was no use. Wilson carefully examined the bat through the net.

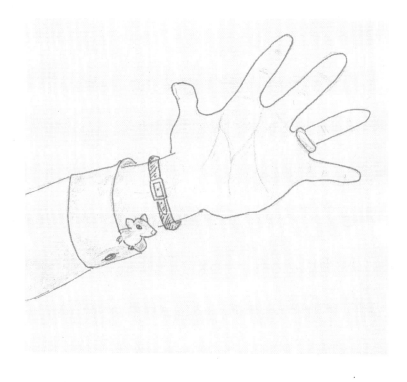

"Hmph! Two heads! What will they go on about next?" He chuckled to himself as he stepped down the ladder to the floor. "Now to get that bucket of water . . . ." He began to whistle as he put the net upside down on a little table by the wall.

Fiona craned her neck to see her terrified friend tangled up in the net. "Don't worry, Bart. I'll get up there somehow!" said Fiona.

"No! Go away," said Bart. "He'll catch you, too. Run for it, Fiona!"

"But I can't just leave you like this," Fiona said. "Hurry, hurry," she whispered to herself.

Fiona clung to the table's wooden leg with her four paws. She leapt and caught the tablecloth with her teeth and front paws. She hung on for dear life.

In the distance water poured into a plastic bucket.

Fiona pulled herself onto the table and immediately began chewing on the net.

She could hear the approaching thunder of the janitor's footsteps.

Fiona chewed and chewed. She had never chewed so hard in all her life. The dusty taste of the net filled her mouth and entered her nostrils. She suppressed the desire to sneeze and closed her eyes, chewing and chewing and chewing until bits of string fell away. Soon there was a hole large enough for Bart's head.

"Close your wings," she whispered, then kept chewing to make the hole larger still.

The whistling janitor set the bucket beside the table and reached for the net.

"Now!" squeaked Fiona as loudly as she could. She crawled inside the janitor's sleeve, slid down his back, and leaped to the floor. This startled Wilson so much that Bart had time to squeeze out of the net and flap up towards the ceiling and into a dark hole.

Wilson the janitor bellowed.

Fiona squeezed under the costume room door, hiding in garments bunched in the corner. She sat there trembling as the hollers and stomping of the janitor continued for what seemed a long time. The shock of it all left her exhausted, and she fell asleep.

Chapter 7

Escape

Bart was out of breath. He found a dark, warm board inside the hole where he could rest.

I could have died! he thought.

Then he thought of Fiona. What courage! She could have been killed, too. Why did she take such a chance?

The humans were not likely to give up. What was he to do now?

He shook his paws. He scratched the spot on the tip of his nose. Then he twittered to figure out where he was.

There was something strangely familiar about this hole. He could not remember ever having been in here before -- or had he?

He pushed his way through drooping tufts of pink insulation to a crawl space between the ceiling and the roof where he could stretch his wings. As he fluttered about this space, cramped though it was, he felt drawn to one spot where the air was fresher. He rubbed his back against a piece of insulation and, to his surprise, discovered nothing solid on the other side.

He pushed through a tiny slit and found himself slipping through to the outside. He flapped up and about, rejoicing at the feel of the cool breeze ruffling his fur.

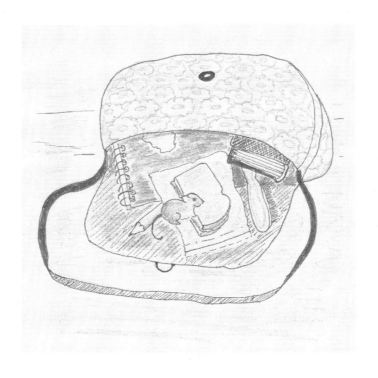

Chapter 8

Hunger in the Mouse Hole

The doorknob rattled. A key clicked in the lock. Fiona stirred beneath the pile of clothes.

Then the outside door opened and a woman marched across the room. She dropped a bulging brocade handbag on the work table. A delicious odor rose from something inside the bag. Fiona could see a bit of plastic sticking out, but even more important, she could smell the salami sandwich wrapped up in it.

Soon more humans bustled about, putting on costumes and making their final adjustments. Not wanting to have another encounter with a human being for a very, very long time, if ever at all, Fiona froze.

She stayed still until most of the actors had left the room, except for one woman who was busy mending the hem of a blue flowered dress. Fiona slid out from underneath the pile of clothing and crept to the crack in the closet door. She paused by an empty coffee mug, remembering her mother's warning to stay away. As she hesitated, another crew of performers tramped noisily in.

Fiona ducked into the closet. There at the very back was the trap, the cheese now dried, but still very appealing to a hungry mouse. Beyond the trap, Fiona could hear the quiet whimpering of her brothers and sisters and the strained warnings of her mother. Fiona thought again about the sandwich still smelling strongly from the brocade handbag.

Then she heard a thump! In their excitement, someone had knocked the handbag to the floor. Fiona scurried towards the bag slumped against the wall. She dove in. She nibbled through the plastic and came away with her cheeks stuffed with sandwich crust. Then she went back to the mouse hole where several pairs of shining eyes stared back at her. She tossed her crusts over the trap and into the hole.

"Oh, dear, dear Fiona!" cried her mother. "Thank you, sweetheart. The children are starving!"

Fiona returned to get another few bites to bring back to her family. She approached the bag. Just as she was getting ready to squeeze inside, a large hand came down and picked the bag up, placing it high on the table top.

Fiona panicked. A few screams arose from the actors as she scampered across the floor away from the closet and through the open door. She ran and didn't stop until she found herself at the back of the stage. She crouched behind a loose board and shut her eyes.

When she opened them, she saw that the entire auditorium was filled with humans, one in each seat. Dancers and singers crossed the stage in a spotlight that shone from a box high on the opposite wall.

Though she knew she was hidden behind the board, invisible to them all, Fiona began to shake.

Chapter 9

Rescue!

The smells and sights danced around the young mouse. She began to hear the same melodies her mother always sang at bedtime to lull them to sleep in the nest. So many of the songs were about love. The villagers were preparing for a wedding feast, and a grave decision had to be made.

Fiona listened from the hole where she sat. She thought about her family starving behind the trap at the door of their mouse hole inside the costume room closet. She thought of Bart who was somewhere unknown, perhaps even gone forever.

In spite of the bustle all about her, Fiona felt all alone.

The room was getting warm with all the dancers jumping about and the actors coming on and off stage. Bright lights shone down on them all. While Fiona sat trembling behind the board, trying hard to figure out what she should do, someone propped open the outside door to get some air moving through the room. Fiona saw a dark shape flap in through the open door.

The green velvet curtain closed while the humans changed the set. Fiona could hear voices still speaking in front of the curtain. She decided to run for it. She scurried along the wall towards the open door. The dark shape swooped down and, sure enough, it was Bart.

"Fiona! I found my way to the great beyond. I've seen my family out there by the big light. There's a wonderful feeling way out there -- wind moving across your fur and lots of things to eat. I wanted to come back and tell you all about it, but I couldn't get back in until they opened this door. Come with me. You'll love it out there!"

"I can't, Bart. My own family is starving. They're stuck behind a trap at the door of our mouse hole," explained Fiona. She started to cry.

"Show me," said Bart. He flapped along behind her as she led the way across the stage to the costume room door, which was slightly ajar. They slipped in while the humans were busy. Fiona stopped before the trap, and Bart perched on the edge of the red high heeled shoe beside her.

"The trap is right here," Fiona said. "My father died in one of these."

"How does it work?" asked Bart.

"Well, here's the wooden part, and here's the metal part. They are joined together with this curvy spring. But I don't really know how it works. Just that the humans try to trick us with smelly cheese because that's something we like to eat."

"They must want you to touch it," said Bart.

"Oh, no, you mustn't touch it! Ma told me not to," Fiona cautioned.

"Of course, your Ma is right. We don't want to get caught in it. But what would happen if we made something else touch it? Let's give it a try."

Bart grabbed a few bows from the pile and dropped all three of them on the trap. They landed with a flutter.

Next he tried tickling the trap with a necktie. Again, nothing happened.

"What about something heavier?" suggested Fiona. She pointed to the red shoe Bart had been sitting on. "This may do it, but can we move it?"

Bart tried dragging the shoe, but it barely budged. "Help me, Fiona," he said.

Fiona scurried to the back of the shoe and pushed and pushed. Bart pulled from above with his strong teeth and the flapping of his wings. Slowly the shoe moved closer and closer to the trap. Bart lifted the heel slightly from the ground and then let it drop. When it hit the metal bar, they heard a loud snap.

"Oh, what's happening?" called Ma from inside the hole.

"Everything's all right, Ma. We've sprung the trap!" said Fiona.

Chapter 10

A Moment of Fame

All seven mice followed Fiona and Bart out of the mouse hole and through the closet door. The actors still in the costume room gasped, dropping their garments on the floor. They watched the parade of mice with the bat overhead flapping the beat. The mouse parade marched out the door, along the hall, and onto the stage.

"It's not far now," said Bart. "Don't let anything stop us."

"We must be brave, children," said Ma. "Keep together now."

Then something else surprised them. A machine by the curtain started to cough out swirls of fog which drifted across the stage. The green curtains were wide open now, and an ocean of human faces peered at them as they stepped into the fog.

"Ooooooooooh!" came several voices from the audience.

Someone in the first row called out, "What an effect! Look at the big mouse! She's pirouetting around the others!"

And it was true. Ma was so concerned her little ones would lose heart and run back that she danced around and around them to keep them in line.

Bart swooped and made a couple of loop-de-loops himself as he led the mice across the stage and out the door to freedom.

Once outside, Ma was delighted to see all her sisters and brothers waiting for her with open arms. They were lined up at the side of the old barn next door, clapping their paws and shuffling the seeds they had gathered for the homecoming celebration.

You see, bats never were very good at keeping secrets, and the bat family living in the barn had been as happy as hazelnuts that young Bart had returned to them.

Besides, everyone knows that mice will generally jump at any excuse for having a party. They really had missed their sister, too, and were glad to see her home.

But the rest of that story we will have to keep for another day. For the little mouse family were finally going home.

Glossary

Here are the definitions of a few words that some students have found confusing. I'm sure I haven't included all of this book's challenging words in this glossary.

Sometimes you can figure out the meanings of words from the context. Learning how to use a dictionary is very helpful, too.

pirouette (pirouetting): a twirling ballet step.

haunches: back legs of a four-legged animal or the area of the backside of a person's body from just above the waist to the thighs.

forage (foraging): look for food; gather food from things you find.

rafters: slanted boards inside the roof of a building that carry the weight of the roof.

bicker: argue or fight using words; quarrel.

garments: clothes.

whimper (whimpering): quietly cry.

brocade: a kind of cloth that has raised patterns, such as flowers, sometimes with shiny gold or silver threads, too.

echo-location: an ability bats have to find out where something is by sending little sound waves through the air. The waves bump against the object and come back to the bat. The bat can measure how far away the object is by how long it took for the sound to come back. This ability helps bats find their food.

Study guide available with discussion questions, games, recipes, projects, word searches, and more! Visit Fiona's Facebook page for more information. www.facebook.com/FionaTheTheaterMouse Come say hello to Fiona!